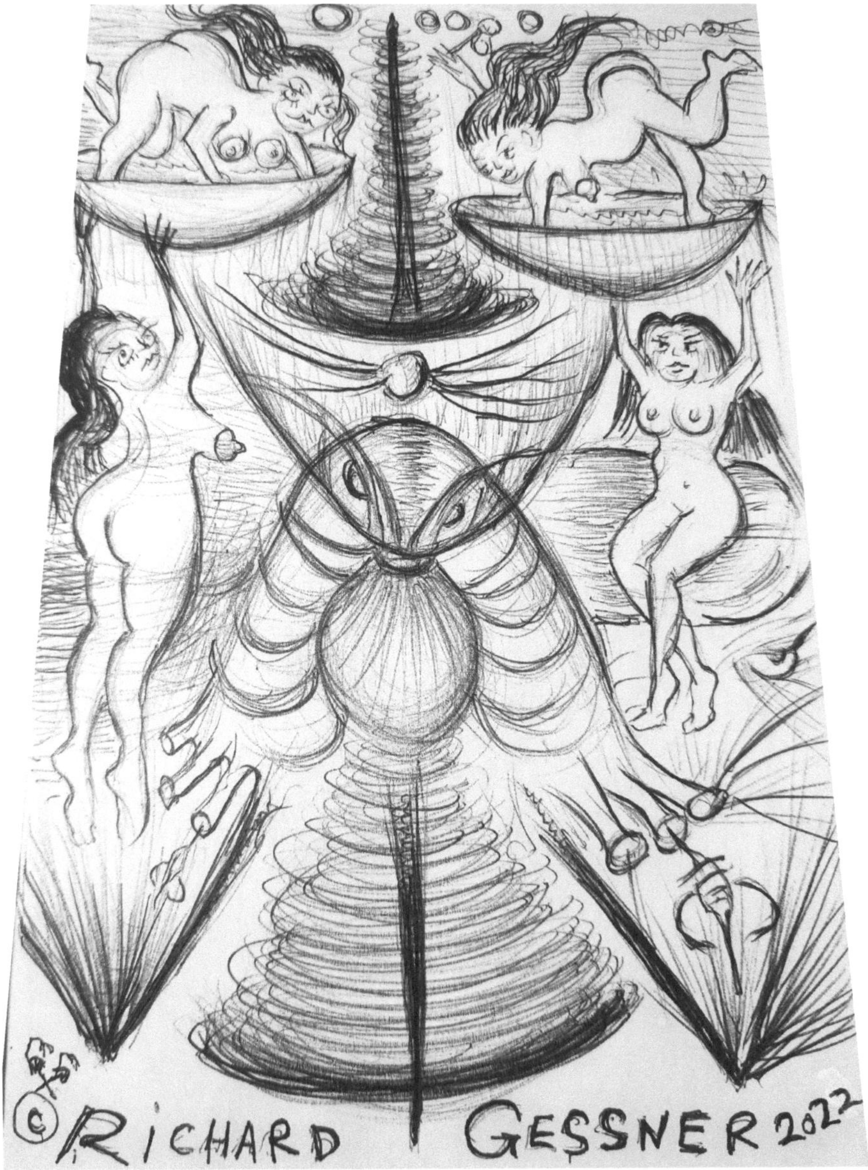

Limulus Whirlpool Nymphs

OTHER PUBLICATIONS BY RICHARD GESSNER

The Conduit and other Visionary Tales of Morphing Whimsy
(print and audio book, Rain Mountain, 2017)

*Excerpts from the Diary of a Neanderthal Dilettante
& the Man in the Couch*
(Bomb Shelter Props, 1991)

Greek In The Wind

SHORT WORKS

Richard Gessner

SPUYTEN DUYVIL

NEW YORK CITY

Grateful acknowledgment to the following magazines
in which this work was first published.

"Greek In The Wind" Seinundwerden
"Fugitive Unborn On The Run" Seinundwerden
"The Hidden Evolution Of Racial Epithets" Seinundwerden
"Triumph At Penis Island" Black Scat Review 24
"The SPAM Of Vegas-Roit" Skidrow Penthouse 20
"Squiggle Fungus Escape Hatch" Dreams & Nightmares
"Voyeur Rising" 3 The Room, Surrealist Magazine, March 2024 Sulfur Surrealist Jungle
"School Chump Memories" Mitchel Pluto Artzine
"Reptile Fling" Mitchel Pluto Artzine
"Orphan Demon Shedding The Skin Of Its Host" Dreams & Nightmares
"Lucky Limulus" Seinundwerden
"Travels Of A Shrew On The Summer Solstice" Sagging Meniscus

ISBN 978-1-963908-64-0

Library of Congress Control Number: 2025937471

Photo on back cover by Rob Pitaccio.

This work is Dedicated to:

Brian McCormick, Vincent Czyz, Doug Schafer,
Mitchell Pluto Uaratiex Mendoza & Joan Sonnenfeld

Contents

Orphan Demon Shedding The Skin Of Its Host

Stalactite Squiggle Contagion

Orphan Demon Shedding The Skin Of Its Host

Stalactite Squiggle Contagion

GREEK IN THE WIND

A Pan Hellenic trinket designed to mollify the curious was given to me by a shadowy agency of relatives of the unknown passing in the night.

The trinket is a translucent diorama of my grandfathers' Diner, 2" long, 1" wide, to fit On a key chain or small novelty display shelf.

As if under a microscope, the chronological history of Panayiotis Stratigakis is visible Through the roof of the miniature diner. Doric pillars on rows of coffee cups vanish in The horizon of countertop covered with displays of spanakopita, kalamata olive, feta Cheese salads and baklava.

When I shake the diner in my fist, tiny figurines of my grandfather light up, linking Arms in a sirtaki dance accompanied by the sounds of a tiny red bouzouki player. Valiently flashing neon lights of blue and white striped patterns of the Greek flag Move up and down the diner, highlighting his personal and national history.

At the front entrance stands the rocky terrain of the Peloponnesian peninsula Where my ancestors have lived for thousands of years. There's 400 years of Ottoman rule, subjugation and bloodshed between Greek and Turk.

A greek ancestors' gold sword slashing the carotid artery of an Ottoman overlord Glows like a beacon of hope, heralding the victory of the Greek war of independence. The port of Piraeus, from where my grandfather sailed to America is then visible, Followed by a heroic image of my grandfather as a tall, handsome young man

Setting foot on American soil for the first time. His rapid rise in socioeconomic Class represented by the elite prep schools where he sent his promising sons. An honorable image of Panayiotis in middle age as a pillar of the community,

A leader in the Greek Orthodox Church glows, emitting rays of light in the Middle of the diner.

Suddenly I notice there's evidence of tampering in the diner diorama. Tiny diagonal fissures crisscross the Clear lucite windows and roof, where Significant parts of my grandfathers' history had been removed.

Paid off micro vandals with precision saws cut out slices of his life, hushed up Buried secrets were blurred, then erased. Walls of shame pancaked on top of Each other, horrid character flaws were sugar coated, and thus rendered Innocuous. The inflamed canker sores jutting from my grandfathers' Conscience, were filed down with chisels then surgically excised.

The crater scars remaining were spackled over with dreamy blue tourist' Brochure views of the Aegean Sea.

I attempt to return my Pan Hellenic trinket to the agency of unknown Relatives, to show them the evidence of tampering, to retrieve the missing Slices of my grandfathers' life, to get a refund or replacement diner diorama, However, the agency of unknown relatives were nowhere to be found.

But soon in the gray dawn of an early spring morning, the missing slices of My grandfathers' life were revealed. Over the cooing of a sandalwood Morning dove, could be heard the voice of my grandfather anglicizing

His last name to Sherwood because Stratigakis sounded too much like Streptococcus. "Streptogakis" had associations which were not good for business.

Or he was hiding and wanted to vanish without trace. Elusive and transient as the wind. In the lucidity of the first daylight, floating on the breeze, was a vision of my Grandfathers' swarthy, muscular body enveloping my pale 15 year old Grandmother, a non-greek girl. It was mere sport to take the girls' virginity, But when she got pregnant, my grandfather vanished, and was never heard From Ever again. My teenage grandmother was burdened with an illegitimate Child she never wanted. My mother had greek features, swarthy olive Skin, dark eyes and hair, like her father. She grew up fatherless. In poverty.

Then it occurred to me to ask Panayiotis Stratigakis "where was your democracy then?"

And to ask "How do you reconcile being a pillar of your community with being a Deadbeat and a statutory rapist?"

But my grandfather was long gone, like my mother, into the eternal beyond. Someone had to bear witness for my mother, because no-one cared or remembered I realized that I was part greek by ill gotten gains. A grandfather who didn't acknowledge his own daughter, my mother.

As I was the grandson of a statutory rapist, son of a bastard; the dishonor Panayiotis cast over my mother was too much to bear. In a misguided attempt at rectification, I Got between many macho greeks and their wives and daughters, provoking them to "fight me like a man"

But the dishonor Panayiotis cast over my mother and her memory still lingered. The Pan Hellenic trinket felt infinitely light on my key chain. But it was heavy with my mother's unresolved conflicts. I was burdened by the weight of it.

The trinket was a family heirloom, as rare as a comet that passes by only every 10,000 years. But I had the need to be rid of it, it didn't mollify My curiosity as the agency of unknown relatives had intended.

To break free of the curse afflicting my family, restore my mother's honor and undo the defilement of my own blood, I cupped the trinket In my left hand and threw it with all my might high into the sky, the Trinket traveling far, vanishing from sight over the Peloponnesian Peninsula in Greece where my ancestors have lived for thousands of years.

Staircase Arthropods

Doric Pillar, Wolverhedgehog

The Hidden Evolution of Racial Epithets

Before the dawn of language, when all utterance was Gibberish, words had no meaning; the first racial epithets Were born innocently as ancient spidery cave drawings.

Scratchy jagged lines depicting tiny insulting hand gestures; Flagellum tangents of middle fingers flipped between Protozoa and parasite, bacteria and amoeba, dramatic strife of microorganisms mushrooming as Intra species slurs amongst the animal kingdom increased.

The colorful bird of paradise calling a common pigeon A dull grey drone. The majestic king cobra, bold and supercilious, calling The humble garter snake a fraying thread from a bankrupt Farmers' shirt. The sleek nimble weasel's smug indifference to the beauty Of the brindle patterns of big cousin wolverines' coat.

Full of potential for expressive hatred and derisive scorn, Smoldering with bad intent; the early racial epithets long Lay dormant; aging poisons fermenting, Larval words Clustering into round, red lace doilies; a devil's needle point.

The forbidden words waiting to be introduced into the Vocabularies of developing homo sapiens. The words Finding their true meaning only after cataclysmic world History played out-rivers of bloodshed flooding 7 continents-casualties of endless wars forming a vast Mass grave of victims and victimizers, reaching beyond Our solar system.

It was then, rising above the transient minutiae of life, The epithets were imbued with power, meaning and Context, having the wide ranging capacity to offend, Cause controversy and discord.

The taboo words came of age, and men were struck Dead by lighting bolts of name calling.

Gangs of racial epithets; clusters of rolling red lace doilies Stampede like outlaw bikers or rabid hyenas, across a thin Skinned landscape as vulnerable as a newborn bunny.

The leader of the pack, King Slur, flashy flamboyant, So offensive it can't be spoken, wears its ugly history Like a badge of honor; King Slur seizes the limelight Having the Alpha status of a fighting word, much Envied by lesser less offensive epithets with fragile Egos.

An epithets' self worth is determined by frequency of use And maximum offense when spoken. Epithets suffer From neglect when for noble reasons they aren't in Someone's vocabulary.

Pity the wimpy slur, bland as tofu or cottage cheese, Which announces itself with a saccharine greeting Card jingle.

Pity the declawed neutered slur, unable to offend, Useless as an old work horse sent to the glue factory.

Pity the obscure, antiquated slur uttered at deaf phantoms In a provincial backwater, not heard and dimly understood By the judgmental ears of a damned civilization.

Beware of epithets that get misconstrued as compliments Beware of moldy tripe past its expiration date.

Beware of sunflower seeds laced with tiny razor blades Beware of sharks as cuddly as kittens.

If someone calls someone a bad word, and atomic bombs Are dropped all over again, take a vacation and sail to Epithet Isle where a pure slur language is spoken by Litigious masses in perpetual offense collapsing in upon Each other as they speak themselves into oblivion and King Slur is smiling and laughing as they vanish.

Die Ungehorsam Kaulquappe

HORSESHOE CRAB TELSON QUINTUPLETS
GESSNER
©2016

Conduit Fish Flowering

Kidney Stone Delerium

Garlic Weevil Tongue Lasso

Vergangenheitsbewältigung

An unborn fetus quietly growing in his mother's
womb became a precocious prolific killer.
tapping into the horrors of the worst of adult
psyches, he made forays outside the safety
of his mother's womb, entering into uncharted
rough territory, ransacking many centuries'
of atrocity, the mushroom cloud of the bad
consciences of condemned men hung over
the fetus guiding him to commit unspeakable
acts. keeping down overpopulation unchecked.

aping the ferocity of the wolverine, he'd stolen
the kills of apex predators in the wilderness.
smiting the grizzly bear, wolf and lion with his
mighty umbilical cord.

with the blink of an eye, he'd wipe out
entire armies already on the road to their
own demise.

in lighter moments, he was the ring and run
doorbell prankster of authorities in pursuit
of the most wanted unborn monster, heralding
the age of genocidal embryo.

by the third trimester of his mother's pregnancy
the fetus was convicted of war crimes in an
intrauterine nuremberg trial. the guilty
einsatzgruppen in his soul glowing red

with bloody hands washed clean by
waves of exoneration in the amniotic
fluid enveloping the fetus returning
to the womb to continue growing and
getting born in a normal birth, leaving the
baggage of karmic destiny of past lives
behind him; blank slate of a baby boy
growing into a married man, living with
his wife and children in a nice house
surrounded by a white picket fence.

Dolphin Larvae

Richard Gessner © 2010
"Teething Trinity"

RICHARD
GESSNER
2019

Triumph at Penis Island

A giant aquatic blue Strongman lies on his back, deep down on the floor of the ocean. The shaft of his huge, long permanently erect penis reaching upward Through the oceans' depths, jutting out from the ocean where waves meet sky.

The mushroom cap of the circumcised glans-penis head is a tropical island paradise the size of Hawaii. Lush palm trees grow, multicolored birds cackle, Feral pigs wander, pink sand dune beaches surround the island populated by Rich sensual swarms of naked ladies living without shame, having never known Clothes.

To pass the time in an otherwise motionless state, flipper feet embedded deep in Coral reef sedimentation, a sunken treasure of manhood, the Strongman with his Strong left hand, is drawing naked ladies on the ocean floor with a brain coral Pencil.

Sinuous lines with skittering crosshatching and chiaroscuro, flow from the massive Exacting left hand, classical renderings form in deep dark still waters, detailed, anatomically flawless drawings reminiscent of 19th century French court painters.

Each drawing is a monument unto itself, indelible. Strongman imbuing every line with a strength and permanence a shark would break its teeth on.

No wayward jealous octopus tentacle could erase them…immune to the mollusks' insult, impervious to the predatory sea urchin banderillas.

No derisive laughter from reform schools of mocking clown fish could thwart the Confidence of the trembling vulnerable lady drawings ascending off the ocean Floor after the strongman's signature signals departure.

Floating upward through murky depths, black, gray, yellow, drawings transforming Into real flesh and blood ladies, swimming upward, unimpeded by bathing suits, marauding sharks smelling their menses get swiftly kicked to oblivion by the Strongman's mighty flipper foot, stronger than iron and thicker than 100 Redwood trees.

The ladies swim ashore at the outer frenulum rim beaches of Penis Island. Welcomed by crowds of naked sisters frolicking in the sunshine, palm trees Swaying in the gentle breeze.

The urethra and pee-hole high on the mountain summit of Penis Island Spews forth a fine blue sperm drizzle into the stratosphere; a randy volcano,

Old faithful geyser of continuous ejaculation—vas deferens, seminal vesicle And urethra working overtime, running on eternal lust.

Many ladies carrying umbrellas and parasols to keep from getting wet as they Stride across the island beaches.

Hailstones of spermatozoa pods bouncing off umbrellas. Pods strewn across beaches which the ladies eat and become pregnant, doing cartwheels giving birth to Litters of airborne baby strongmen carried like milkweed threads on the winds blowing them far from penis island. Some are destined to grow into giants who Become alpha penis islands of their own.

Down deep on the ocean floor, the Strongman feels the constant pitter patter of Feminine feet upon the head of his phallic member, ladies keeping him in a permanent state of arousal—maintaining homeostasis on the island, sunken Treasure of manhood drawing naked ladies on the ocean floor...

Feral Donut Boy

BACK
BRiSTLE ELiXiR ®
BACK
BRISTL
Richard GESSNER © '08

GESSNER © 2005
"HORSESHOE CRAB
TELSON
QUINTUPLETS"

His mother had a very long pregnancy, gestation period spanning out Across decades. Nino was finally born full grown, taking his first breath Well into middle age.

Hence he had no childhood, no growth, no puberty, no maturity, he didn't Age. Always a spanking newly minted coin of a boyman with a diminished box of a body.

He couldn't aspire to being castrati, because he was born without balls to cut off. He didn't salivate for girls and no girls salivated for him.

Nino bore the distinction of being the prized petrock traded Amongst Egyptian Pharaohs, the doorstop of mighty dictators, a paperweight for architects of the timeless eunuchs of future generations.

Baby giants used him for shot put practice. Redefining the lowest level of the pecking order, Nino had been the valet of humble bait boys Carrying buckets of worms, following in servitude behind jaunty Fishermen.

Some neighborhood Italians, sanded down the four corners of the Box boy, playing Bocceball with him in a local park. The sanded Corners grew back,Nino reverting to his box shape when the game Was done.

Once, I passed Nino on the street, reflecting that over 40 years Ago- in school we had sat next to each other in Mrs. Parks' Spanish Class, further reflecting that he'd had the coordination of a stalwart

Slug on barbiturates in Gym class, and that to pin him in a full nelson in the wrestling room was no challenge. That I'd rather shoot fawns With a pea shooter. Or paint phantom polka dots on plastic daisies.

Nino reared upon one corner of his box, selfrighteously exclaiming "Richard! You're living in the past! You have to be a contemporary Guy like me!"

The town rockstar's fame cast a very long shadow, a wedge of darkness with a Bermuda Triangle wherein dwelled the rockstar's younger brother castrated and erased by the rock star's fame.

It was here the unearned "Specialness" of being born into rock royalty festered into a canker sore of obnoxiousness, pretense and over Compensation. Afflicted with the curse of being ordinary, the rockstar's younger brother asserted his uniqueness by spelling his very common Name in a very uncommon way, so you'd never forget he was a rare bird of paradise.

After school, at 4 o'clock, groups of us passed a Marijuana cigarette between us, and the rockstar's younger brother, in a haze of smoke, summoned the visage of his famous brother, his fame eclipsing

The heads on Mount Rushmore the Shining Sphinx, the grandiose heads of state in eternity, a Mummy of the first hominid preserved at the Earth's Core.

Gleaming scalpel in hand, Dew Drop Envy, casually diced up his crucified Dissecting frog in Biology Class. Vandal meat for which he'd receive a D on his report card. Energetically, Dew Drop Envy proclaimed his ambitions to become a pimp or an assassin if he never graduated from high school.

Dew Drop Envy, a poor kid, who gravitated toward rich kids, is often reemembered lounging in lawn chairs, sipping strawberry Daiquiris at posh suburban pool parties. On occasion, he'd get lucky with the soft and pliable girls of the upper class shedding their clothes with Ease to swim in the moonlit pools of stately mansions.

The mirage of a giant, multicolored phosphorescent Dung Beetle Rainbow appeared on the horizon of my Home Town. The huge hind legs of the Dung Beetle forever rolling up a mediocre saxophonist wearing his High School Marching Band coat in late middle age—a regressive laughingstock—held in limbo.

For generations, the Dung Beetles' hindlegs gripping him firmly never letting go as he spins him in circles; an intergenerational curse which can't be broken as he performs gauche acts, bringing outside food into Restaurants, playing tawdry music for chump change.

poop chute, parachute, somersault, sleep

Richard Gessner © 2010   "Fabelwesen Frühstück"

The SPAM of Vegas-Roit

A hunk of SPAM the size of Jupiter has supplanted the earth. The SPAM is an imperial sponge—soaking up the world's oceans—absorbing the continents—

Growing the temperate desert suburb of Vegas-Roit, hanging precipitously off the cliff of luncheon meat like a neon satellite appendage.

The SPAM glistens, a faded industrial pink pariah of the universe, casting massive pork by product shadows, oozing in bubbling gels, shimmering in cloudy blue halos of sodium nitrite emanating from The timeless but slippery planet.

Millions of cars have been driven into the SPAM's surface over the Millennia by countless unknowing drivers flooring their gas pedals To take a shortcut to the SPAM's core.

The SPAM is spiked with cars of every make: Pontiacs, Buicks, Cadillacs, Lincoln Continentals, Volvos, Trans ams, Alfa Romeos, Olds Cutlass Supremes, Jaguars, Corvettes, Mitsubishis, Thunderbirds, Hondas, Mazdas, Mercedes, Mustangs, Dusters, Isuzus

Are projecting from the luncheon meat like multicolored metallic Quills. An aerial view of the SPAM is a mosaic of back bumpers, fenders, windows, trunks and tires speckled with a patchwork of license plates from every state of the union.

The mummified drivers who crashed through their windshields ages ago, are smiling and tranquil, embedded in the hardened dried meat just beyond their steering wheels, dashboards and front Bumpers.

The mosaic of car spikes is linked by a vast web of chewed spat out bubblegum, a pink sticky vine stretching over the expanse of rear bumpers, winding its way through tire treads, trunks and fractured chassis, curling around, reflecting in the mirrors of the bumpers, sizzling and bubbling in the salty neon air of Vegas-Roit.

Here and there, a stalactite of congealed butter hangs off a bumper,

Bubbling over at its narrow most tip with the clogged blood vessels And high blood pressures of many Vegas-Roitian.

Vegas-Roit, a hybrid Las Vegas and Detroit, is a homogenized Suburb of identical split level box houses built from the crumbled Reprocessed remains of car factory assembly lines, hotels, motels, Gambling casinos, nightclubs, bars bordellos, instant divorce Agencies, coat hanger abortion clinics and porno theaters.

In place of the earth's extinct vegetation, is a desert of broken Glass-cotton candy-fiber glass sand, dotted with tumble weeds Of wool fallen prematurely from flocks aging pink wrinkled Lambs wandering through an orange grey landscape.

On the front lawn of each house is a stuffed used car salesman Lawn jockey holding a glistening alumnium key once used To open cans of SPAM back in the good old days when it was packaged in cube shaped metal cans. The lawn jockeys are testaments to the age of gluttony, quaint kitsch relics Of a bygone age, contemporary talismans and reminders Of the inevitable exodus of which no Vegas-Roitian can Escape.

In the mirage of an aurora borealis laced with the ghost of Photosynthesis past, millions of Vegas-Roitians will burrow Into the SPAM in a gluttony rush, furiously eating away At the exposed areas of meat between car spikes, Mercenaries Stampeding over each other in a competitive race to the SPAM's Core.

GESSNER ©'07

Alpha Ducky

BACKBRISTLE ELIXIR®
CUNNILINGUS PINKY PUPPETS®
RICHARD GESSNER ©'09 "OFFSHORE DRILLING"

Alpha Ducky

BACKBRISTLE ELIXIR®
CUNNILINGUS PINKY PUPPETS®
RICHARD GESSNER ©'09 "OFFSHORE DRILLING"

Die Auferstehung

RICHARD
GESSNER
© 2022

Voyeur Rising

Strategically positioning his beach chair, pretending to be reading a Daily newspaper, Joey Genauski, nonchalant, invisible, just by chance, settles in a tight rectangle of sand bordering the burgundy beach towels of two 19 year old college girls the age of his granddaughter.

The Girls, an ash Blonde, and a Brunette with auburn highlights, have Soft buttery skin, shapely, wide hipped—all curvaceous splendor—Perfect brown bodies striped with pale tan lines sharply outlining pale Pink asses and naturally large breasts jiggling slightly in the warm breeze of early summer.

The tanlines form a pale faded triangle V of panty line extending upwards From butt crack to lower back, panty lines curving around thighs to below Belly buttons—traces of cast off bikini no longer worn.

Gradations of pale pink skin merging to olive, cinnamon, golden brown, Pale breasts encircled with D cup outlines of frilly brassieres. Burnt Sienna areoles and nipples a darker shade of brown than their overall tans.

Crisp yellow and gold designer bikinis, light summer Dresses, brassieres And panties are strewn across towels covered with tubes of sun screen, Purses, car keys, fruit, sandwiches cold drinks, a paperback of classic 19th century literature and a current glossy fashion magazine glistening in the sun.

Furtively, through dark sunglasses, Joey Genauski gazes longingly Towards the girls' spread open legs. Their Smoothly shaven vaginas, A reddish salmon pink, are soothed with cooling aloe vera.

Blue and white beach umbrellas with a swordfish logo line the beach Landscape. Its a Saturday afternoon in early June, the weekend Crowds work to Joey's advantage, giving him an excuse to sit close to single women without being obvious about it. The crowds camouflaging His true intentions, allowing him to move frequently, unnoticed by the

Morally reproving beach patrol seeking to squelch his habit of constantly wandering the beach in quest of a perfect view.

Other voyeurs, Joey's competition, watch the beach entrance from a Distance, waiting for the arrival of young ladies, single or in groups. Approaching the ladies after they have gotten naked under their beach umbrellas.

Most women strip naked, but some keep their bikini bottoms on. Some wear Brazilian string bikinis, flesh toned thongs, almost nude, But not quite. Pale maidens wiggle out of floral print summer dresses, Shorts, and candy striped one piece bathing suits.

Voluptuous brown girls peel off demure, white see-through-when-wet Suits, revealing all to bulging male eyes, looking, gawking, looking away—Diaphanous mesh panties slide down svelte hips, falling to sand.

Brightly colored, fancy brassieres pop off as Delicate fingers reach behind Unhooking clasps shining in the sun, catching the eye of a seagull flying in blue skies above.

Secret cameramen get up in the nooks and crannies of spread eagled Women half asleep in the sun.

Joey leaves the two girls, vanishing into thick masses of beach regulars, middle aged, tanned and leathery, marking their territory with Windscreens, Coolers and little plastic flags poked in the sand.

In Joey's absence, competing beach voyeurs, some bold, well hung, Smooth talkers, will succeed in engaging the Ash Blonde and Brunette with auburn highlights in a lively conversation. Mastering Bare Body language A virile stud will advance to slow massage, rubbing baby oil on their perfect Bodies glistening in the sun.

Slick voyeurs who remain at the top of the food chain will return to the beach, summer after summer, appearing like clockwork as in The legendary return of swallows to Mission San Juan Capistrano—Their pick up routines with the ladies will remain similar and predictable Year after year, decade after decade. Enticing the girls with superficial big talk of financial conquest, fancy cookies and little airplane bottles Of alcohol.

In the tidal pools of voyeur nursery school, untested new generations Of voyeurs emerge like baby sea turtle hatchlings making a mad dash seaward—climbing the slippery slope of a succulent female ass just over the Horizon.

Joey Genauski wanders into a gaggle of girls taking it all off for the First time-In the distance, randy couples frolic in the surf, avoiding the June Jellyfish in the waves, out at sea, fishing boats come in close to shore, catching a Panoramic eyeful of skin.

The Matador's Reprieve

Spiny Turkey Foreplay

Tumescent Turkey Glory

Lucky Limulus

An aboriginal Horseshoe Crab in an oceans' childhood puddle, measured its species' millennia of daybreak—Tracing itself back, before time began—

Book lungs of arthropod covered with a relief map of pre-hominid fingerprints, marking each breath with a motif of anonymous mass signatures—

Overlapping faceless spirals, recording time like age rings on a sawed off cross section of redwood tree stump.

Blue blood Limulus, royally surviving earthly extinctions of fauna ephemera, surpassing all competitors with unchanging form—

Priapic Telson shooting skyward; phallic tail mating with Princess Polaris, begetting north star children of jellyfish, plankton and sharks.

Squiggle Fungus Escape Hatch

GESSNER ©   2013

Die Ungehorsam Kaulquappe

GESSNER © 2013

Die Ungehorsam Kaulquappe

Travels of a Shrew on the Summer Solstice

A shrew, still young, but aging fast, took its last breath On the summer solstice.

The insectivores' short life span and the longest day Of the year converge time frames.

Life sped through the shrew faster than the resurrection Of a still-born fruit fly.

The sun didn't set. Tomorrow hovered on the cusp of midnight.

A transient paramecium, mistaking the shrew for the Wallet of a millionaire, got its one cell stolen by a pickpocket surfing a fleeting twinkle of life.

A loan shark and an old maid elope, using the shrew as a marriage license-

Bound together in expedient chastity, they bribe each other with spinster dollars, having a steady appreciation in Value.

In sand castles washing out to sea, old and young dust motes of insectivore beget tidal pool shrews, shiny and newly minted in a short breath of time replenishing itself.

Richard GESSNER © 3-27-2023 0000

Reptile Fling

I took Maryellen, a lady of leisure, to every expensive restaurant And high end bar, indulged her with gourmet food, fine wine and droll conversation.

I spent a lot of $ on her, as a Gentleman always pays for a Lady. It was my intention to wear down her defenses and inhibitions, To spend a day and night with her, warming her up to strip naked in a luxurious hotel room with a heart shaped Jacuzzi.

Maryellen was a glamorous, statuesque beauty, with creamy platinum blonde shoulder length hair, pale pink lipstick and nail polish. She wore a demure antique white designer dress, shimmering nude nylon stockings, and strappy high heels. Her ample breasts, curvaceous shape and nice ass, were her most noticeable feminine assets.

Maryellen was the kept woman of a film producer who was her Sugar Daddy. She was useful as eye candy at public events, and made the producer look good. She lived rent free and got a generous allowance for other "services" Too shadowy to mention.

Maryellen was a precocious Sugar Baby, adept at sucking The blood of Men with deep pockets. I was also friendly with the film producer who owned two summer homes and drove a Jaguar and a Mercedes. I had business dealings with the film producer of an artistic nature. But having no loyalty to him, I jumped at the opportunity to get his girl if I was lucky.

By chance, I met up with Maryellen, while passing through the Producer's neighborhood, and it was then that she went on several surreptitious dinner dates with me. She welcomed time away from her Master who was overbearing, controlling and played power games with money. Threatening to withhold funds from her when he didn't feel sexually satisfied.

But Maryellen was successful at twisting the producer's arm to buy her a new high end designer purse, not some cheap fake discount.

A giant alligator sex toy swallowed Maryellen whole and pooped her out its butt into the Florida heat, designer handbag and all. A giant alligator sex toy swallowed Maryellen whole pooping her out its butt, soiling her designer clothes, making her sad.

A giant alligator sex toy swallowed Maryellen whole, she found spiritual enlightenment in the alligator's digestive tract, emerging naked from the reptiles' butt, and in her nakedness, she was most comfortable in the Florida heat.

All erotic, exotic and grotesque epiphanies aside, after many expensive dinner and bar dates, I finally got Maryellen to spend a day and night with me in a luxurious hotel room with a heart shaped Jacuzzi. After she took off her demure designer dress, stockings and heels, I helped her out of her panties and unhooked her brassiere, then she lay naked on the bed and I rubbed eucalyptus oil on her body. Then we entered the Jacuzzi together, in the warm water she blissfully felt my stiff erect phallus entering the prime real estate between her legs.

RICHARD GESSNER ©2010
"ROOTOPUS SUCKLE"

Duelling 5 leaf clover on swollen left pinky promontory

© 2022 Richard Gessner

RICHARD GESSNER ©2010
"ROOTOPUS SUCKLE"

Duelling 5 leaf clover on swollen left pinky promontory © 2022 Richard Gessner

In a quiet town in Bavaria, two patriotic snails who had come of age during An Easter holiday, were moving down the street past a candy store window Where inside a hierarchy of a thousand chocolate bunnies were sitting in rows Like the Nazi party meditating on their future plans.

The snails stretch their antennae upwards in salute to the bunnies. The labels In the shirts of passers-by on the street, fall onto their antennae as armbands. Tiny developing frogs in the labels twist into swastikas.

The snails get confused because some of the bunnies are dark brown, others Vanilla white, making them look like an integrated public school outside the Third Reich.

Surely the "Master Race" would not approve of this, thought the snails glancing at each other apprehensively. They continue to watch the hierarchy For a long time.

One of the bunnies in the front row is leaning against the candy store window pane, its blue sugar eyes watching the snow capped mountains in the distance as its body melts, becoming quite deformed like the foot of an infamous Propaganda Minister.

When the snails notice this, they dutifully go next door to a shoe store to shoplift some orthopedic shoes. They hide on cans of black shoe polish so they won't be seen by shoe salesmen kneeling at benches holding the feet of lady customers. When the snails find the orthopedic shoes they drag them outside with their antennae wrapped around the shoe laces.

A bunny leaning against the candy store windowpane has melted down Into the shape of the lining inside the shoes. Its blue sugar eyes stick To the windowpane, watching the snow capped mountains in the distance.

The snails salute the blue sugar eyes with their antennae, crying mournfully for their nations' future loss. Tears crystallizing at antennae tips like transparent frog's legs. Patriotic crying sounding like a tadpole's veins becoming aware of legs sprouting on either side of its shrinking tail.

The owner of the shoe store hears the crying and comes out onto the sidewalk, angrily putting on the orthopedic shoes and walking towards The Police station, the snails dangling from the shoe laces as though in handcuffs.

At the police station they are forced out of their shells with night sticks. The police crawl inside the snail shells with flashlights, as the snails dangling from the shoe laces look like dilated pupils or shorn black poodles.

The Chief-of-Police puts on the orthopedic shoes, doing a handstand on the floor of his office, dipping the snails in an ink bottle on his desk. When the barefoot shoe store owner gives his nod of approval, a sergeant and a lieutenant then untie the snails from the shoe laces, pressing them against white paper, taking their antennae prints.

The sergeant and lieutenant re-handcuff the snails to the shoe laces of the Chief-of-Police who walks them to a fish bowl jail cell, full of water and a tiny glass toilet.

The shoe store owner asks the Chief-of-Police to return the orthopedic Shoes but he refuses. The shoe store owner walks back to his store, Barefoot and shivering, attempting to stare down the blue sugar bunny Eyes sticking to the windowpane watching the snow capped mountains In the distance.

The snails wait in the fishbowl jail for a lawyer to be assigned to them by The court. Their empty shells gather dust on the police chief's desk along with machine guns, bombs and knives seized from criminals over the years.

The snails get very bored, sliding around in circles on the glass toilet Seat to pass the time. Years pass, a lawyer never comes. In time, the

snails have their shells returned to them. They wear them pretending
They are war helmets.

   Often they hide their antennae shamefully because they could not
Serve their country fighting in the war. The snails grow old, their Shells
streaked with grey, antennae wrinkling like sterile milkweed threads.

   They spend their days sliding in circles on the glass toilet seat, dis-
cussing The "Master Race" reminiscing about their childhood skiing
down mountains on the tips of their antennae.

   One day, an albino fetus, resembling a monstrous dictator was ad-
mitted to the fishbowl by the Chief-of-Police. The stodgy, long institu-
tionalized snails watch it swimming around, mistaking it for the appa-
rition of a Teutonic burlesque dancer, umbilical cord trailing from is
belly like a sheer white corset.

   The fetus's brain floats out of its head through its nostrils and eye
sockets, the snails hearing the faint roar of the ocean inside its hollow
head like a sea shell. The brain drifting around the fishbowl is a pow-
der puff for the burlesque dancer to apply her rouge and eye liner.

   The brain returns to the safety of the hollow head when the snails
become boisterous like men at a burlesque show. Once, the brain
emerged from the fetus's ear, causing a solar eclipse in the fishbowl.

Morphing Strongmenn

Squiggle Competition

LuckyLimulus
RichardGessner
© 2022

Dung Beetle Conspiracy

Flagellum Paradise